For mice everywhere, A.McQ.

First published in Great Britain in 2000 by Zero To Ten Limited
327 High Street, Slough, Berkshire, SL1 1TX

Publisher: Anna McQuinn
Art Director: Tim Foster
Senior Editor: Simona Sideri
Publishing Assistant: Vikram Parashar

A CIP catalogue record for this book is available from the British Library.

ISBN 1-84089-181-5

Printed in Hong Kong

"This won't take long..."

Austin McQuinn

Mimi adores her new blue vacuum cleaner.

Every Saturday morning she starts in the living room.

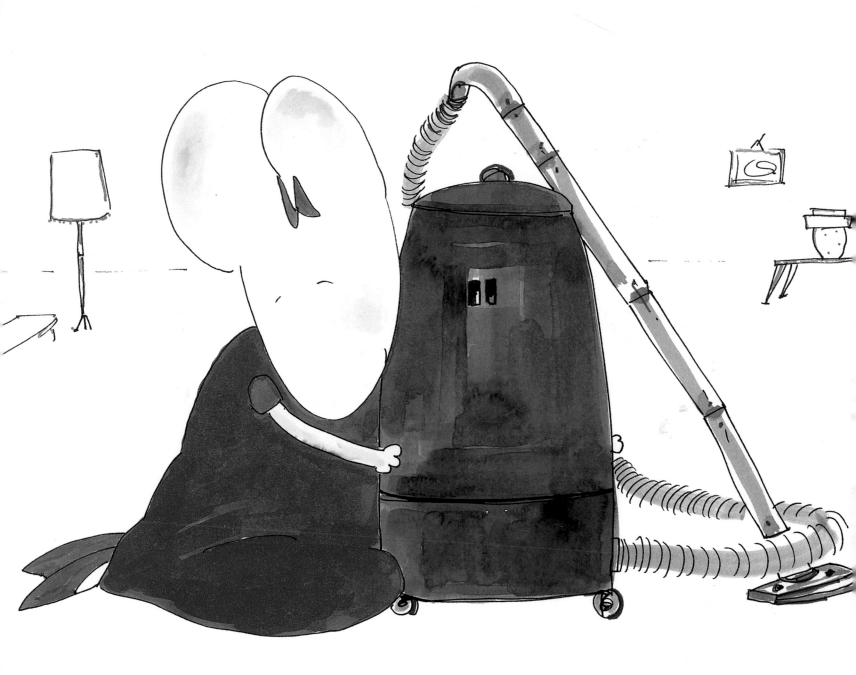

Under the table she finds a green button.

"Oh, that's where it went!" says Mimi.

"This won't take long..."

And she takes out
her sewing things.

"That's great!
Now, back
to work,"
she says.

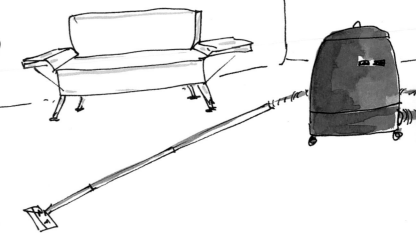

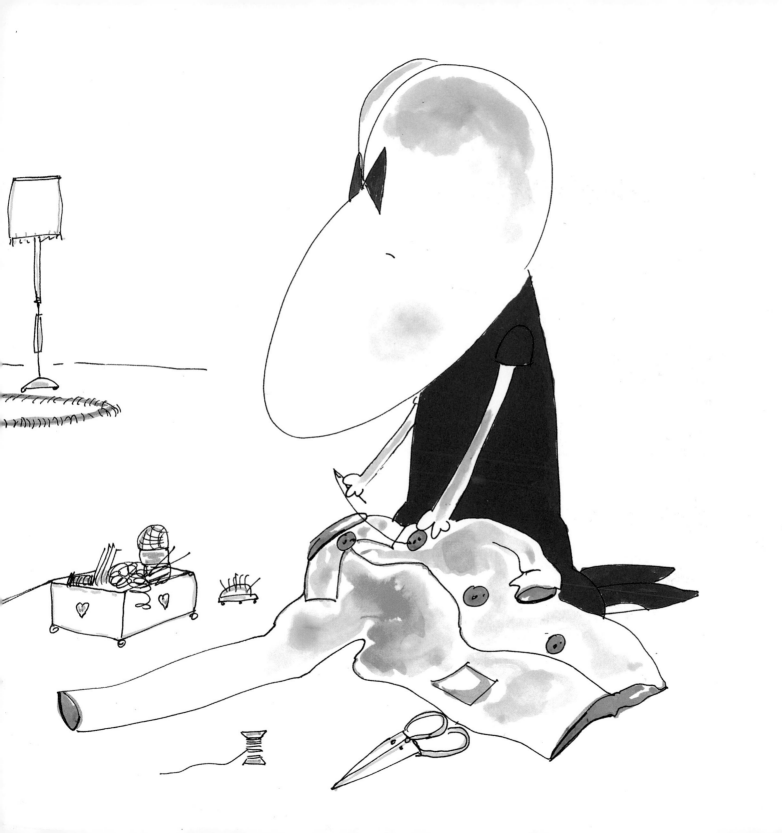

Behind the curtains, Mimi finds her favourite pink pen.

"So, that's where it's been hiding!" says Mimi.

"This won't take long..."

And she sits down
to finish her letter
to Claude.

"What shall I put at
the end?" wonders Mimi
as the phone rings.

"Yes, Monica of course come to lunch. I'll make a soufflé.

It won't take long..." says Mimi.

Mimi whips up a soufflé
and pops it in the oven.

On the floor
she spots her book.

"Superb!" she says,
"and only a few
pages left...

This won't take long..."

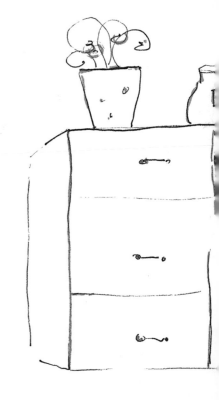

Then she notices
her yellow bow.

"At last!" says Mimi.
"Now I can wear
my yellow dress!

This won't take long..."

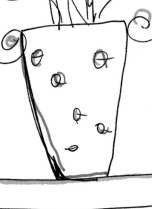

In the pocket,
Mimi finds a sweet.

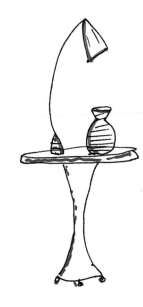

"Mmmmmmmmm...
Toffee..."

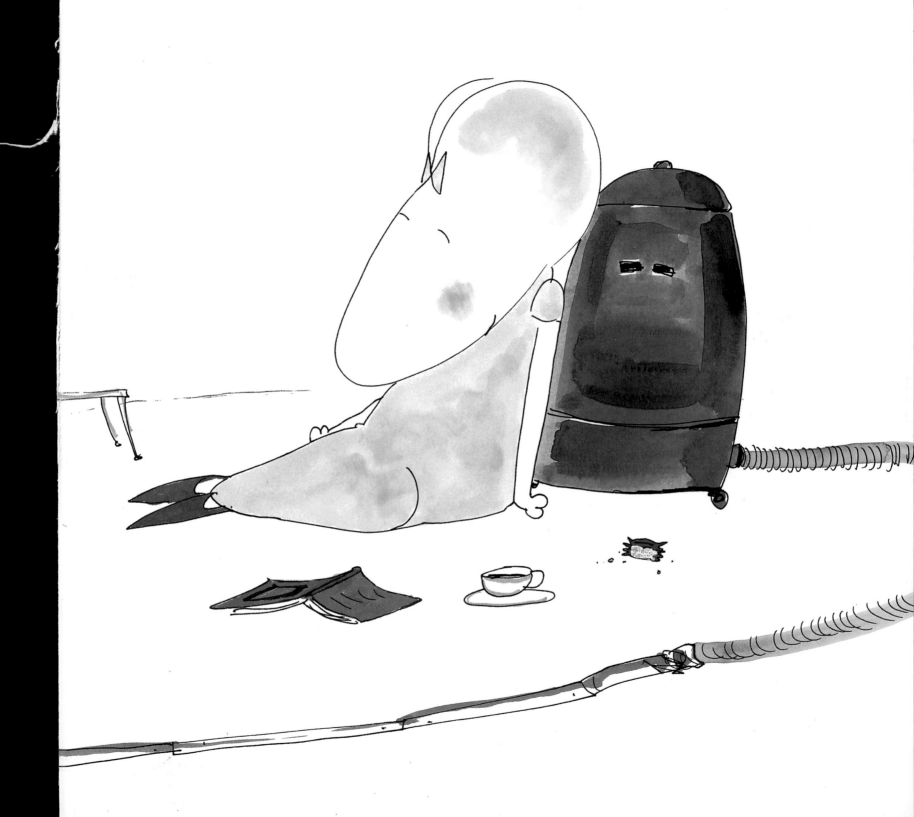

Ding Dong -
"The door!
It's Monica already!"

Bing -
"The oven! The soufflé
must be done."

It's ENORMOUS!

"Lunch is going to take ALL day!"

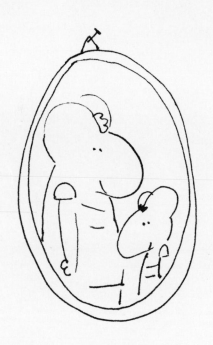